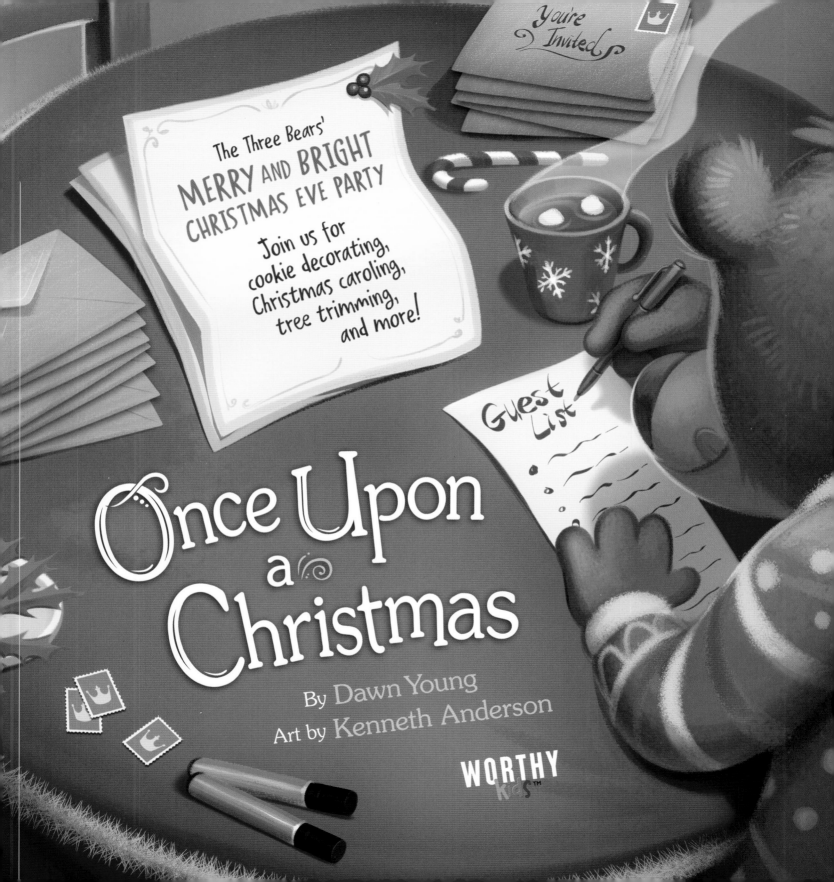

The Three Bears'
MERRY AND BRIGHT
CHRISTMAS EVE PARTY

Join us for
cookie decorating,
Christmas caroling,
tree trimming,
and more!

You're Invited

Guest List

Once Upon a Christmas

By Dawn Young

Art by Kenneth Anderson

WORTHY
Kids™

Once upon a Christmas, the Three Bears decided to host their first-ever Christmas Eve celebration.

The Bears planned and prepped, down to the last detail, so everything would be *just right*. They invited everyone in the land.

You're Invited

The guests dressed in their Christmas best and gathered at the cottage.

The party was full of festivities: baking, building gingerbread houses, Christmas caroling,

AHH-CHOOOo!

trimming the tree,
taking photos,
and reading
Christmas stories.

Too close

Too far

But nothing went as expected, and just when the Bears thought things couldn't get any worse . . .

Rapunzel tumbled onto Jack Frost, knocking the wind out of him and causing the squall of the century.

Whish! Whoosh! Swish!

The gust ripped down wires and blew out lights. It whipped through the windows. Ribbons, wrappings, and wreaths scattered everywhere.

All was *not* merry and bright!

Meanwhile, on the other side of the woods,
Santa was making deliveries when—

Whish! Whoosh! Swish!

The sleigh spiraled
down, down,
down, until . . .

Splash! It plunged into Baby Bear Lagoon, and Santa stood waist-high in water.

"Ho! No! No!" exclaimed Santa.
"The presents! I must get them delivered."

He set out to search for help.

Santa shivered as he sloshed through the woods. Soon, he spotted a house.

He tapped on the door. It opened, so he went in.
Immediately he found three pairs of pants,
three pairs of socks, and three pairs of boots.

"Ho! Ho! Ho!
Much better,"
said Santa.

Then, all of a sudden,
he heard quite a clatter.

He raced down the hall
to see what was the matter.
"Jolly jingle bells!"
shouted Santa.

Papa Bear, spying his
pants and boots, growled,
"Somebody's been—"

"Ho! Ho! Ho! I know," said Santa. "I'm so
sorry. I was soaked, and now I need help.
My sleigh is stuck in the lagoon."

"Of course!"

Everyone scurried to help.
The Gingerbread Man ran
as fast as he could, and
the others followed.

They drew up a plan.

The mermaids rescued the
sack and brought it to shore.
Bigfoot and the Giant waded
through the water and pushed,
while the others pulled.

At last, the sleigh slid out.

The Not-So-Big-Bad Wolf *huffed*
and *puffed* and blew the sleigh dry.
Once everyone gathered the stray
presents, Santa's sleigh was ready to go.

Together, the team saved Christmas!

The Giant chanted, "Fee-fi-fo-fum,
let's head back and have some fun!"
and led the parade back to the party.

Before he dashed away, Santa
stayed for cookies and cocoa.

The festivities were
in full swing:
baking, building
gingerbread houses,
Christmas caroling,

trimming the tree,
taking photos,
and reading Christmas stories.

This time, all *was* merry and bright
on a blanket of white.

Then Santa said, "Ho! Ho! Ho! Time to go!
It's getting late, and I have a lot to do."

"Can I help?" asked Little Red.
"I'm already dressed for the part."

Everyone waved goodbye, and they heard
Santa exclaim, as he drove out of sight,

"Merry Christmas to all.
May your day be
just right!"